Malia
in Hawai'i

AUTHOR'S DEDICATION
To Meg, Will, Gem, and Sam ...
my kamaʻāina keiki.

ARTIST'S DEDICATION
For precious Kairi, whose smile
brightens the world.

ISBN: 978-1939487-19-3

First Printing, October 2013

Mutual Publishing, LLC
1215 Center Street, Suite 210
Honolulu, Hawaiʻi 96816
Ph: 808-732-1709
Fax: 808-734-4094
email: info@mutualpublishing.com
www.mutualpublishing.com

Printed in China

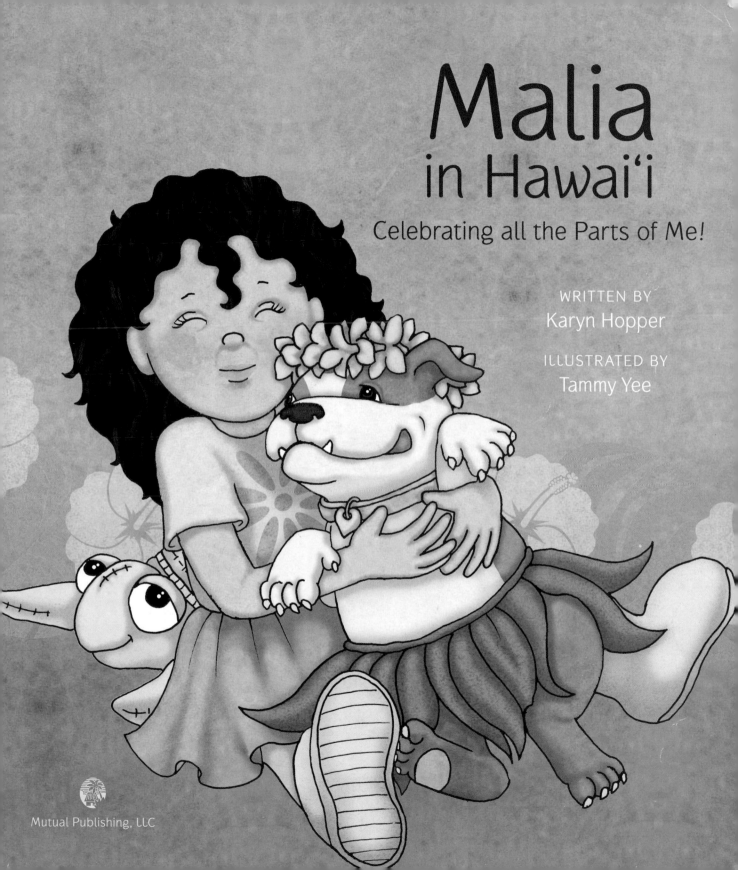

Malia
in Hawai'i
Celebrating all the Parts of Me!

WRITTEN BY
Karyn Hopper

ILLUSTRATED BY
Tammy Yee

Mutual Publishing, LLC

Malia **Sachi** Ging Ging *Lee* ...
If you could choose, who would you be?

One-finger, two-finger, three-finger paste,
Malia loves the taro taste.
Steam it, pound it, scoop the poi,
Malia says it's "nō ka 'oi!"

Japanese sushi, sesame seed,
Cucumber, crab, and dry seaweed.
Roll it, dip it, on your dish.
Sachi's favorite is the fish.

Halo, halo, cold and sweet,
Coconut milk and fruity treat.
Munch the mung beans,
crunch the ice.
Ging Ging loves the
pounded rice.

Stir-fried, crispy, cold or hot
Noodles fill *Lee's* empty spot.
Slurp them, gulp them from a bowl.
Lee likes chow mein best of all.

Malia Sachi Ging Ging Lee...
If you could choose, who would you be?

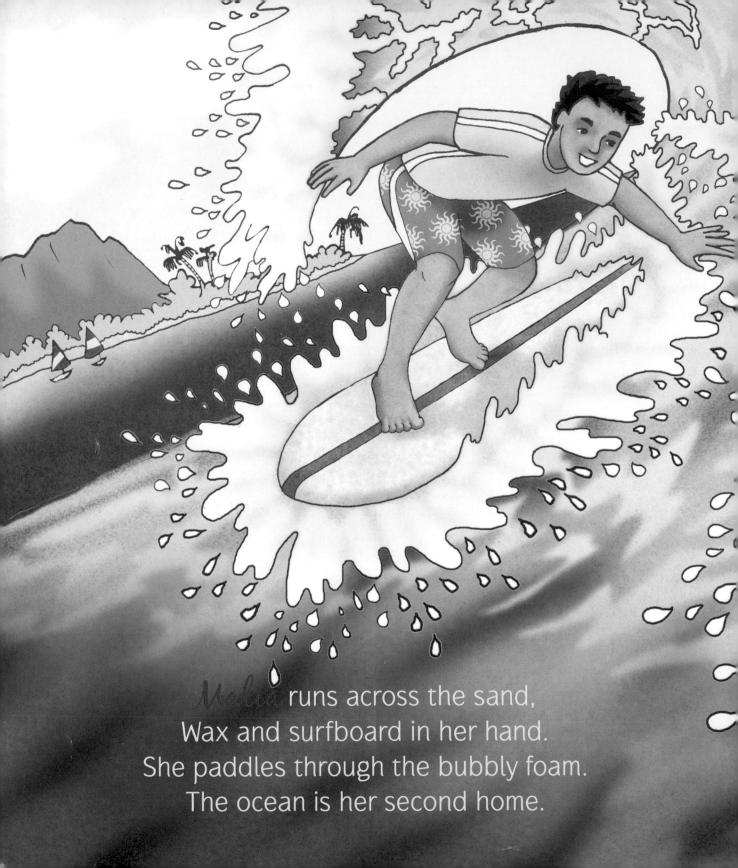

Makoa runs across the sand,
Wax and surfboard in her hand.
She paddles through the bubbly foam.
The ocean is her second home.

Jan-ken-po, I cannot show!
Sachi choose, but don't be slow!
Throw down paper, throw down rock,
Throw down scissors for a block.

Tinikling, tinikling, tap, tap, tap!
Filipino dancing, clap, clap, clap!
Bamboo poles slide on the ground.
Ging Ging's feet move to the sound.

Chinese jump rope, grab two friends,
One as center, two as ends.
Lee hops over, out, and in,
Makes an X and starts again.

Malia Sachi Ging Ging *Lee*...
If you could choose, who would you be?

Malia threads a flower lei
To celebrate the first of May.
Swaying hips and dancing feet
Keeping time to hula beat.

Sachi's dolls are dressed with care,
Kimonos bright and costumes rare.
Girl's Day means it's time for fun,
Tea and treats for everyone!

Uncles, aunties, cousins, too,
Fill the house with gifts and food.
To the noise of laughs and shouts,
Ging Ging blows her candles out.

Bright lights shoot across the sky.
Fireworks pop a loud reply.
Dragons dance to *Lee's* loud drum.
Chinese New Year has begun.

Malia

Sachi

Ging Ging

Lee...

Put them all together and
YOU ...HAVE ...ME!